Jackie,

Best Wishes!

To Lesley for sharing my passion, giving me strength, supporting my endeavors, being my love and also my best friend. You inspire me to be me and are the reason this is a reality. ----PJP

For Amy, Samantha and Sierra ---- MG

Tree Of Life Publishing
1001 Avenue of the Americas
12th Floor
New York, NY 10018

Published by Peeper & Friends, an imprint of Tree Of Life Publishing 2006.

Printed in Hong Kong.

Library of Congress Control Number: 2004104401

Parente, Peter
Peeper Goes To Florida / by Peter Parente: illustrated by Michael Graham

ISBN 0-9745052-1-8

Peeper Goes To Florida

Story By
Peter Parente

Illustrations By
Michael Graham

As the sun went down he sprang up, wide-awake.
"Florida bound, but what means of travel will I take?

Land will take too long and airplanes are not for me.
Looks like the only option left is to travel by sea."

"This small sailboat will be perfect for the seas.
Excuse me, Mr. Fish, which way to Florida please."

"I'm actually not a fish, but an air-breathing mammal like you.
Today's your lucky day. You can ride with me if you want to."

"My name is Peeper, the kinkajou. I'll join you if you don't mind.
Thank you for your offer and for being so kind."

"I'm Flash, the bottle-nosed dolphin. I'll be your guide in the sea.
The ocean can be dangerous, but you'll be safe with me."

"My sonar keeps track of everything beyond my sense of sight.
Shelly, the sea turtle, is tangled in a net and appears to be losing the fight."

"If you swim me in close I can try to untie the knot.
We have to take a chance. We're the only hope she's got."

Flash swam Peeper in and they were able to get Shelly free.
"Sea turtles are endangered because of what just happened to me."

"Here comes Max, the hammerhead shark, looking for a snack. Be sure to stay close to me so I can watch your back."

"A turtle and a furry treat would have been great.
Be thankful you're with Flash or you'd be shark bait."

"Well Max, I hope we didn't ruin your day.
Kinkajou might give you heartburn anyway."

Max swam off. Flash and Shelly escorted Peeper to shore.
"They seem like a nice family. Just knock on their door."

"They are as nice as they look and have
been known to get me out of a rut.
Once they untangled me from fishing line
and then they cared for my prop cut."

"Peeper this is Manny T and he is one of the local sea cows.
He is a great guy, but has been hit by too many boat bows.

Welcome to the island of Key West, where we are all from.
Call us by the water when you are ready. We'll be sure to come."

When Peter and Lesley opened the door to their surprise,
Peeper gave a peep and looked at them with cuddly eyes.

Peter turned to Lesley and said with a smile,
"We can let him stay in the guestroom for a while."

Howie, the mutt, could not care at all.
He was busy playing with his ball.

But Winston, the pug, did not agree.
"He is going to be trouble. Just wait and see."

Peeper slept and he slept and he slept some more.
They put him in his room for the night and shut his door.

Little did they know when they laid down to sleep,
the mischief Peeper was capable of without the slightest peep.

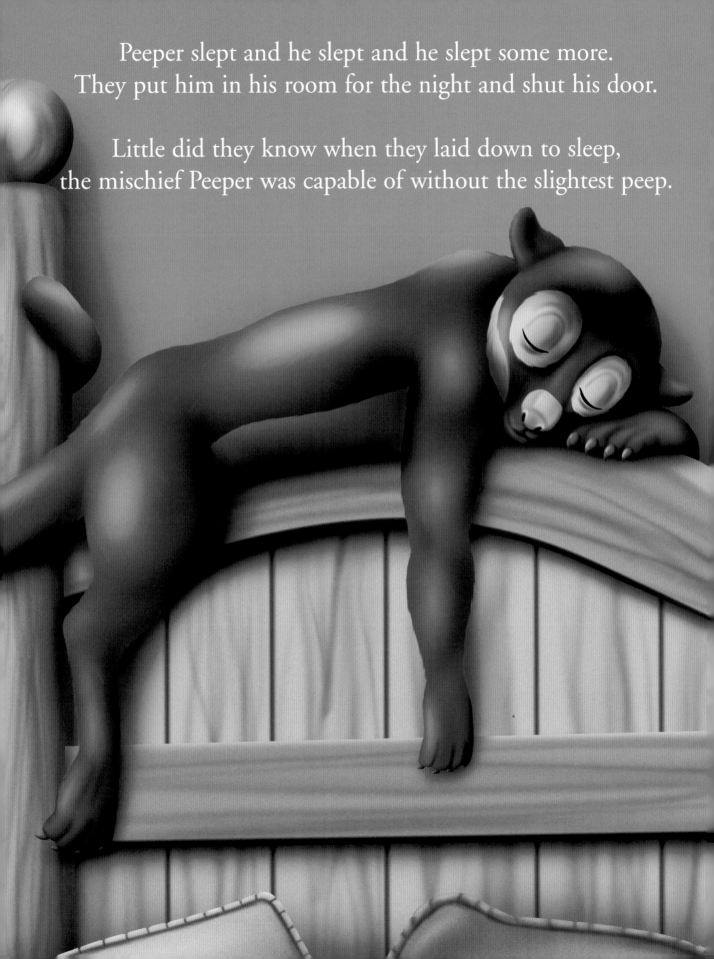

He jumped up, turned the handle, and opened the door.
He could hear Winston sleeping with his loud pug-like snore.

He slid down the railing, across a shelf, then to the floor.
Winston and Howie wondered what was in store.

Peeper opened the cabinets with all the food.
Now this kinkajou was in an even better mood.

"Look at the mess you started to make.
You've eaten potato chips, cookies, and cake."

"I did not mean to make a mess and be so rude.
I got really excited about the different types of food.

Where I live, I only get insects, fruit, and leaves to eat.
All these different foods were such a splendid treat."

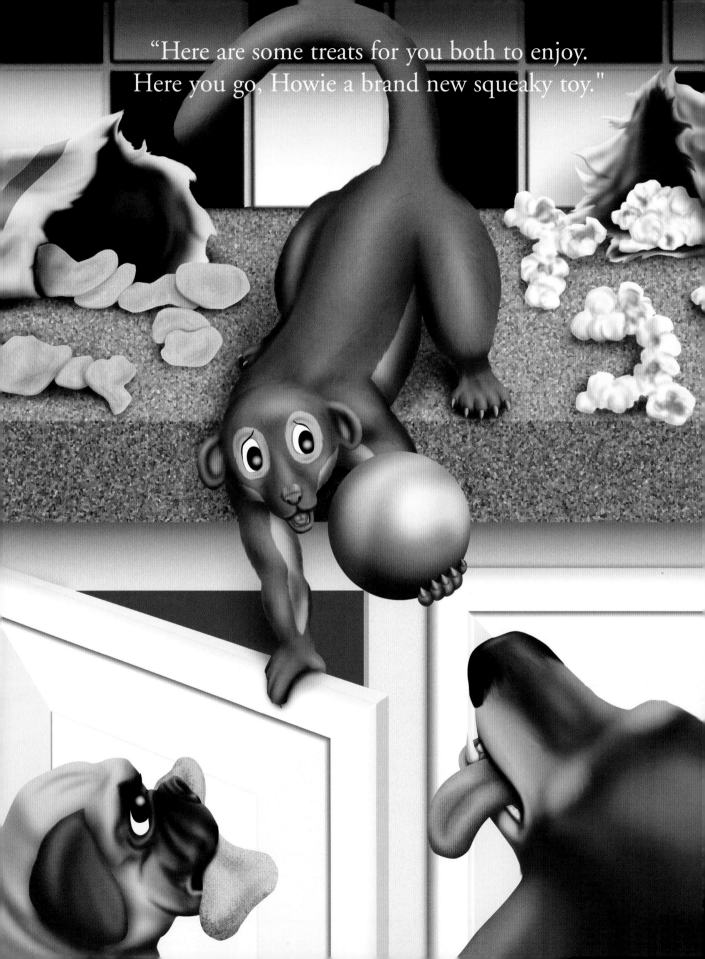

"We need to clean up this mess before the end of the night.
Get all the empty boxes, cartons, and wrappers out of sight."

After cleaning the house they got to know each other.
Winston and Howie made Peeper an honorary brother.

Winston and Howie spent the next few nights with their new friend
They were going to miss Peeper when his vacation came to and end

Peeper enjoyed his trip to Florida, but really missed his home.
The rainforest was where he was meant to roam.

They were sad to see him go, but happy to make such a friend.
They all knew this would not be...

The End

Author Peter Parente gets an up close introduction to Kibby at Dolphin Research Center

Dolphin Research Center was founded as a not-for-profit corporation in 1984 on Grassy Key in the heart of the fabulous Florida Keys. Home to a family of Atlantic bottlenose dolphins, California sea lions and assorted other creatures, we are an international tourist destination and one of the most highly respected education and research facilities in the world. DRC is proud to be an accredited member of the Alliance of Marine Mammal Parks and Aquariums.

Our mission is to promote peaceful coexistence, cooperation and communication between marine mammals and humans and the environment we share through research and education. The health and well being of DRC's dolphins holds absolute precedence over all other interests. We will undertake no program or activity that compromises this basic commitment. Through the years, we have operated as a critical care center and a retirement home for animals from other facilities. We are funded entirely by the admission and program fees paid by the people who visit our center, and by private donors and members.

Every day, we offer continuous half-hour presentations in which we share the fun and excitement of dolphins in action, while also providing important information about the animals and the need to protect the ocean environment. We also offer a variety of interactive programs including our week-long, college-accredited DolphinLab, our Dolphin Encounter structured swim, our DolphinSplash wade-in program and several other opportunities to meet the dolphins from the dock. Dolphin Child Therapy provides new gateways of learning through therapeutic, goal-oriented dolphin interactions. We are handicap-accessible and can provide individualized assistance for guests with special needs.

Dolphin Research Center is the only licensed manatee rescue team in the Florida Keys. Our trained assessors and rescuers respond to upwards of 100 calls per year on entangled, injured, sick or orphaned manatees from Key Largo to Key West.

By becoming a member of Dolphin Research Center, you will help us care for our family of dolphins and sea lions, plus support our rescue work with the endangered Florida Manatee. Membership options range from Adopt-A-Dolphin to Individual Memberships. All options include free admission to DRC, in addition to other benefits. Please visit our website, www.dolphins.org, for complete information.

Dolphin Research Center
58901 Overseas Highway, Grassy Key, FL 33050-6019
www.dolphins.org